Bialosky's Special Picnic

By
Leslie McGuire

Illustrated by
Jerry Joyner

Created by Peggy & Alan Bialosky
A Golden Book • New York
Western Publishing Company, Inc., Racine, Wisconsin 53404

ISBN 0-307-02018-5/ ISBN 0-307-60290-7 (lib. bdg.)
G H I J

Bialosky woke up early. He stretched and got out of bed.

He brushed his teeth, fluffed his fur, and went into his kitchen to get breakfast.

Breakfast was honey, of course.

"Every morning I brush my teeth and fluff my fur," he said as he reached into the cupboard for his honey pot. "Then I reach into the cupboard to get some honey for breakfast."

He took the top off his honey pot and sat down. "I wish today could be different," he said. He stuck his spoon into the honey pot.

He took the spoon out of the honey pot. It came out empty. "Oh, bumblebees!" cried Bialosky. "Today is already different, and I don't like it!"

Bialosky sat and thought. He thought about his empty tummy, and he thought about his empty honey pot.

Then Bialosky had an idea. "I'll go to the woods and find some wild clover honey," he said. "And I'll make a lovely picnic lunch to take with me!"

He thought some more, and then he said, "And I'll ask Suzie to come, too."

Bialosky put on his overalls and tied a bandanna around his neck. Then he went back to the kitchen.

Bialosky opened his cupboard and looked at the things inside. There wasn't much. There was a pile of nuts. There was a lemon. There were some crackers. And there was a picnic tablecloth.

Bialosky put all those things into his picnic basket. He still needed something to hold the honey he would find, so he took his empty honey pot, too.

Then he set off for Suzie's house.

"I'd love to go on a picnic," said Suzie, looking at Bialosky's basket. "Are you sure we'll find some honey, though? A picnic isn't much of a picnic without honey, you know."

"Don't worry," said Bialosky. "I brought some other things along, and I know exactly where the honey is."

So off they went through the woods. Soon they came to a little lake, and sitting on the shore was a little boat.

"Let's borrow this boat and row to the other side," said Bialosky.

They got in, and Bialosky started to row. When they reached the middle of the lake, Suzie shouted and picked up her feet.

"This boat is leaking!" she said.

Bialosky looked down. Indeed the boat *was* leaking. It was leaking a lot.

Bialosky had just enough time to put the picnic basket on his head. Then the boat sank.

"Well, at least our picnic didn't get wet," he said as they sat drying themselves on the shore. "Our food is safe."

At that very moment, a long line of ants was marching out of the grass. The ants walked right into the picnic basket. Then they walked right out the other side . . . with *all* the crackers.

Bialosky didn't notice. "Let's start looking for the honey, so we can have our picnic," he said.

They looked in the big trees.

They looked in the small trees.

They walked farther and looked longer. But they found no honey at all.

"Are you sure we're in the right woods?" asked Suzie.

"I'm getting hungry," Suzie said at last. "Why don't we eat our lunch while we're waiting for the rain to stop? We'll have honey for dessert."

"Good idea," said Bialosky.

“A lemon!” Suzie said when she looked into the basket. “Is that all you packed for lunch? What kind of picnic is this?”

“I packed lots of other things,” said Bialosky, peering into the basket. “I can’t imagine what happened to them all. Oh, this is a terrible day! Nothing has gone right since breakfast. We’re wet and hungry, and now we have no food.”

"Bialosky," said Suzie, "don't feel bad. Look over there." She pointed through the trees. Bialosky looked and saw the sun peeking out from behind the clouds. The rain had stopped, and there was a rainbow in the sky.

"My mother always told me there's a pot of honey at the end of a rainbow," said Suzie. "Let's go look for it!"

They followed the rainbow out of the woods, down a road, and right up to . . .

. . . a general store with a special sign out front. The sign said, "Honey Sale Today Only."

They bought a big jar of honey and went outside.

Suzie took the lemon from the picnic basket and squeezed lemonade into two cups of water. She put in honey to make it sweet. Then she and Bialosky sat on the porch and drank lemonade and watched the clouds drift away.

"This was a nice picnic after all," sighed Bialosky.

"Well, anyway," said Suzie, smiling sweetly, "it was different."

They sat under a tree and waited for the rain to stop. A little squirrel came down the tree. She quickly popped into the picnic basket, and quickly popped all the nuts into her cheeks. Then she popped back out and up the tree.

As they walked and looked, the sky was growing darker and darker. They walked a little faster. But walking faster doesn't keep it from raining, and soon the rain came pouring down.

Bialosky pulled the tablecloth out of the picnic basket and put it over their heads.